D1497782

Rachel and the Lion

Published by:
Stephanie Lainez
P.O. Box 1471
La Mirada Ca 90637-1471
www.stephanielainez.com
www.cleardrink.cc

PRINTED IN CHINA

ISBN 10: 0-9820358-0-2
ISBN 13: 978-0-9820358-0-1

Cover Design and Illustrations by Megan Stringfellow
Interior Design by Rosamond Grupp
Graphics Designs by Joshua Swodeck

Publisher's Cataloging-in-Publication
(Provided by Quality Books, Inc)

Lainez, Stephanie.
    Rachel and the lion / by Stephanie Lainez.
      p. cm.
    SUMMARY: Seven-year-old Rachel lives in a small African town with no running water and few cars. She has a large family and her parents work hard to create a good life, amid poverty and illness. When her mother dies from malaria, Rachel's friendship with a lion gives her strength and courage to live with her grief.
    Audience: Ages 5-15.
    ISBN-13: 978-0-9820358-0-1
    ISBN-10: 0-9820358-0-2

    1. Poor girls--Africa--Juvenile fiction.
    2. Human-animal relationships--Juvenile fiction.
    3. Bereavement--Juvenile fiction. 4. Africa--Economic conditions--Juvenile fiction. [1. Poor girls--Fiction.
    2. Lions--Fiction. 3. Bereavement--Fiction. 4. Africa
    --Fiction.]   I. Title.

PZ7.L15657Rac 2008   [Fic]
                       QBI08-600221

Rachel and the Lion

STEPHANIE LAINEZ

To my beloved husband Robert.

*Thank you for always being
my Knight in Shining Armor!*

I am truly blessed!

Table of Contents

CHAPTER 1

Face To Face With A Lion

Once upon a time, there was a young girl who lived in a small town—a town with no running water, no toilets and very few cars. Her family was hard working. Her father walked every morning to the end of town where a truck picked him up and took him to work. It dropped him back off late each night. Her mother stayed at home, making sure that the family was properly cared for, that the home was attended to and that meals were made. Then there were the children: Sophie, the baby at about four months old; Joseph, who was two; the twins, Tomas and Tulie, who were five; and last, but not least, was Rachel. Rachel was seven.

She was very small in frame and stature. She wasn't like the rest of the family. Though the whole family was hard working and diligent to serve one another, Rachel saw more, wanted more and hoped for more. She was joyful, even when things around her weren't perfect. She was tenacious and determined. She was silly, opinionated, argumentative and mischievous. Rachel loved to sing and dance. She would skip everywhere and laugh. She was bubbly. She knew how to live. She knew how to love.

Not everything was easy for Rachel. She had

her own obstacles to overcome, and, yes, at seven years old she had seen a lot of things. She didn't go to school, mostly because there wasn't a school near where she lived. She knew how to read a few words but not enough to read a full sentence. She didn't know all of her ABCs—she didn't know fractions—she didn't know what the new fads were—and she didn't know what make-up was or how to use it. She was constantly sick. Sadly, she saw a lot of friends and family die of the same illness. But even still, Rachel had the strength to smile. Her smile was her secret weapon and no one could take that away from her. Even though she was small, she was powerful!

Every morning before her dad woke up, she'd slip out of her dingy pajamas and climb into her faded, green tank top and her pink skirt with the white torn lace along the edges. It was a great skirt for twirling. She'd quietly slip on her torn, dusty, black tennis shoes with no socks and would sit and watch her mother prepare the morning meal. Her mother would sing as she cooked, with Rachel joining in as they danced around the fire that was out back. Those mornings were very special for Rachel. And every morning was just the same, a cooking lesson from Mom, a song, and a dance.

After her father was done with his breakfast, Rachel hurried out to the front of the house to surprise him. Every morning she hid behind the same tree, jumped out, and shouted, "Boo!" And, even though he knew she was there, her dad always acted surprised! She loved him, and the two of them walked to the town's end hand-in-hand every day.

And each day Rachel waved good-bye until she could no longer see the flume of dust from the pick-up truck that would take her dad to work.

The town where Rachel and her family lived sat at the base of a group of hills and mountains. After walking her dad to the towns' end to go to work, Rachel headed off the beaten path, taking a climb up to the hilltop to sit at its peak and wait for her best friend to join her. Sometimes her best friend would be there before she arrived, waiting for her. Other times Rachel would sit and wait for a long time for her friend to arrive. But regardless of the time it took, she never left until she was able to spend time with her dearest friend.

Now, on this particular morning, Rachel was feeling a bit ill, huffing and puffing as she climbed from rock to rock. She began to get out of breath and started to perspire. Drips of sweat made their way down her forehead, falling into her eyes. She wiped them away and noticed beads of moisture collecting on her arms and legs. She was getting tired, but Rachel was determined to get to the top of the hill.

With every step her tiny little legs grew weaker and weaker. She began to shout, saying, "I can! I can! I know that I know I can!" Rachel wanted to spend the morning with her friend, like she had every other morning. But *this* morning seemed to be the hardest. As she reached the top of the hill, little Rachel lost her footing and began to slide down, scraping her knees as she slid. It was then that a big tear welled up in her eye as she looked up to the top of the hill and realized how far she had fallen. She thought that maybe today would be the first time that she and her friend would not get the chance to meet. But Rachel wasn't going to stop. She began to climb the jagged rocks again. Now with the scrapes beginning to sting, a tear fell from her eyes, hit the hot rock and rolled down into the deep red dirt.

Rachel hung her head and began to cry. She didn't want to give up! *I'm not a quitter,* she thought to herself. Then suddenly she felt a tug on the back of her tank top. Out of nowhere the tug lifted Rachel off the ground. She quickly looked to the left then to the right. *How is this happening?* she thought to herself. As she looked down she could see the tips of her dirty black tennis shoes hover over the sharp rocks, and she was surprised to find herself being gently set on the hilltop. She turned around quickly, confused as to what had just happened. And, as she turned, standing there before her was the biggest lion that anyone had ever seen. He was gigantic. His paws were bigger than Rachel's head and his claws looked very sharp. His muscles were protruding, making deep ripples in his fur. She knew he was strong. The fur around his head was deep brown at the root, and his thick mane was dusty and blond. His coat was brown, blond and red. And his face was serious, scary, and intimidating.

Rachel wasn't afraid at all as she jumped at him, threw her thin arms around his thick, strong neck and said, "I thought I wasn't going to see you today! I started to cry right when you lifted me up! You did lift me up, right?"

Lion turned to Rachel and said, "Why would I let you fail? I heard your tear fall before you even knew that you were going to cry! Did you think that I would leave you there crying by yourself? I am the king and I will never leave you! Even when you think that I'm not here, *I am here.* Don't ever forget that!"

Rachel just hugged Lion as her tears fell onto his blond fur. And it was there that she fell asleep, lying across the paws of her very best friend.

As the morning sun grew hotter, a group of zebra ran across the base of the hill awakening Rachel. She lifted her head, finding herself still nestled nicely on Lion's paws. She looked up and heard him say, "Good morning, Princess. I hope your nap was restful." And, as she smiled at him, he lowered his head and licked her cheek. He knew that she loved that. Rachel threw her head back and giggled. "I love you, Lion." she said.

And Lion nodded his head and said, "I love you too, Rachel."

Right On Time

The next morning Rachel's mother asked Rachel if she was ready to cook by herself. The girl's little eyes grew large and, with a lump in her throat, she replied, "Uh . . . sure." Her mother handed her the rice jar, a pot, and a mixing spoon. Rachel looked up at her mother and was nervous. "What if I burn the food?" she asked with concern. Her mother just smiled. "That's why I'm here," she told her daughter. "I won't let you burn it. I'll teach you how to make perfect rice." Rachel was relieved. As the rice reached perfection Rachel's face was beaming with victory. "I did it! I made perfect rice all by myself," she said.

Her mother handed Rachel a plate and asked her to serve her father. Rachel was honored as she held the plate in her small hands and spooned onto the plate a hardy serving of rice. She walked over to the table and placed it in front of her father who looked at her and asked, "Did you make this, Rachel?" Rachel turned and, with a giant smile on her face, gave a thumbs-up to her mother as her mother smiled back at her. Rachel turned back, looked up at her father, and with a big strong voice said, "Yup! I made it all by myself!"

When her father finished his breakfast he

rubbed his belly and declared, "That was the *best* breakfast I've ever had!" Rachel was so proud of herself.

After breakfast, Rachel walked her father to the town's end. As they stood there at the end of the road, her father knelt on one knee with tears in his eyes and kissed her on her forehead. Rachel looked at him and said, "Why are you so sad?"

He smiled and said, "You're growing up so fast. Watching you and your mom cook together makes me proud." Rachel's face was beaming. Her father knew how to make her smile. She squeezed his hand, he jumped into the back of the truck, and they waved good-bye.

As the truck drove away Rachel could sense

that something else was going on. *Why was my father crying? This is different. I feel sad. I guess I'll ask him tomorrow,* she thought to herself. So she turned around and began to skip toward the hill for her morning hang-out time with the lion. As she walked off the dirt road another truck passed, and, as it did, a group of boys jumped out and started shouting at Rachel.

"Hey, you!" shouted one of the boys.

"Yeah, wait up, we got something for you!" shouted another boy.

Her heart began to race as she started to run toward the hills. She could tell that these boys weren't very nice. She knew that if she was close enough to the hills that Lion would see her and would rescue her. But here she was too far away for Lion to even sense any trouble.

Rachel's legs where much shorter than the older boys. She couldn't run as fast as they could, so very quickly they caught up. They surrounded her as they began pushing and shoving her back and forth. She could tell which boy was the meanest. It was the older boy; his face was cruel, his eyes looked sad. His hair was short and very dirty. She could see the dirt on his face and dry grass pieces in his hair. His arms were just as dirty with scrapes and bruises on them. His pants were filthy, too, with big holes at the knees, and he wasn't wearing shoes. She thought that he must be the leader because he was the only one with an old blue bandanna tied around his forearm.

She shouted to him, "What do you want from me?"

He calmly said, "We want your shoes."

"My shoes?" Rachel said. "They're torn, dusty, and they have no laces!! They won't fit you anyway! Why are you picking on me?"

The other boys turned, chuckled and looked at the leader as he began to get even more upset. "I said, I want your shoes so *take them off!*" he shouted at Rachel.

The other four boys laughed as they continued to push Rachel around. The older boy gave one good push which sent her to the ground. She slowly stood up. Her face was dirty and her pink skirt was full of thick red dirt. One of the younger boys began to feel bad as he saw Rachel start to cry. He said to the older boy and their friends, "Hey, maybe we should leave her alone. Let's go pick on somebody else."

"Are you kidding me?" the leader yelled. "This is the most fun we've had in days. Look at her, she's so afraid! Don't you love it?"

"But, come on . . . She's dirty and so small. What's the fun in that? Come on, let's go," said the younger boy.

The older boy became very angry. "We're not going anywhere without those shoes!" He grabbed Rachel and as he clenched his hands around her thin arms, suddenly an eerie, frightened look swept across his face. The wind began to pick up and dirt began to swirl in the air, making a strong whirling sound.

"Um…guys. Umm, what's going on?" he said in a scared and shaky voice. His grip loosened around Rachel's arms. The other boys looked around and didn't see anything. Suddenly the younger boy began to panic. He began screaming loudly and pointing. His face went pale and his eyes grew very large. He looked like he'd just seen a ghost. The other boys quickly grew very scared and started looking around, but, in their fear and confusion, they saw nothing.

The leader said, "What's wrong with you? What're you pointing at?"

The younger boy screamed, "It's a lion!"

The boys looked around frantically and shouted in unison, "What lion?"

Rachel turned slowly as she saw Lion standing there. He stood calm, upright, and majestic.

The boy said, "That *lion*! Don't you see him?" He turned around and ran to the truck with the other boys in close pursuit.

Rachel plopped her bottom on the red dirt in confusion. Lion walked over and nudged her with his nose. "Are you okay?" Rachel just sat there in awe. Big tears began to roll down her face. Lion lay right beside her and said, "Come on, climb on and let's go!" She very slowly grabbed onto his blond mane and gently pulled herself onto Lion's back.

As they were on their way to the hilltop she tugged on the lion's mane and said, "Lion, may I ask you something?"

"*Sure.*"

"Why couldn't *all* the boys see you?" Rachel asked.

Lion just laughed and said, "Well, Rachel, only those who know me as king can see me. That younger boy, he was the only one who knew me. He knew what they were doing was wrong. The other boys felt my presence, but they could not see me."

Rachel said, "I'm confused. I don't understand."

"That's okay, Rachel. You will. You soon will," and, as Lion said that, they reached the plateau. They both sat there together in silence.

I'm Watching

The next morning Rachel woke up and followed her same routine, but this time there was going to be a change in her plans. Rachel was dressed and started to walk out the door to help her mother with the morning meal when suddenly she heard her father say, "Rachel, not today."

"What? Why not?" Rachel asked in disappointment.

Rachel's father sat at the kitchen table as he

put on his shoes and said, "Rachel, today I need your help. Mom is not feeling well, so I need you to be the lady of the house. You need to feed your brothers and sisters and do the wash. Have Tomas and Tulie help you with the laundry."

Rachel looked devastated. She wasn't going to hang out with lion on the hilltop. What would Lion think? Would he think that she had forgotten?

She looked at her father with her big brown sad eyes and said, "Father, I have this friend I visit every morning after walking you to the town's end. I'm afraid if I don't go my friend will think that something is wrong!"

"Rachel, I understand, but not today. I need you to stay home today. Your friend will have to understand," said her father.

Rachel hung her head and murmured, "That's not fair . . ."

Her father lifted her head with his hand and said, "Now that's enough. I need you here. I don't want to argue with you. Just do what I've asked you to do." He stood up from the table, rubbed the top of Rachel's head and said good-bye.

Rachel walked into the bedroom where the rest of the kids were still asleep. She leaned over and lightly shook the twins. They wiped their eyes and looked up at Rachel. Tulie smiled, closed her eyes and fell back to sleep. Tomas kept his eyes open and said in a dreamy voice, "Huh..."

Rachel shook them again, saying in a very

bossy tone, "Mom's sick, and Dad said that you two have to make breakfast for us and the rest of the meals too, and I'm suppose to help you do the wash!"

Tomas and Tulie both sat up and said in a bit stronger voice but still half asleep, "No way! We're too little. We don't know how to cook! Rachel, you're lying! He didn't say that!"

Rachel stood up and said with a firm shout, "I'm just telling you what I heard, so hurry up because I'm hungry!"

Rachel stormed out of the room leaving Tomas and Tulie sitting there dumbfounded. Tomas pulled off the covers and told Tulie, "Come on, we better get started!"

32

Tulie just sat there as big tears began to fill her eyes. "But Rachel's lying, Tomas!"

Tomas stood up and said, "You're probably right. Let's go tell Mom." So they both got up and changed into their clothes.

Meanwhile Rachel was playing on the swing that hung on the tree outside. She was singing away without a care when suddenly she heard a very big strong voice say, "Rachel!"

She jumped off the swing and quickly spun around to see who had called her. And there, standing tall, was Lion. Rachel scurried over and shuffled him to the side of the house as she looked around and whispered, "What are you doing here? Someone is going to see you and then the whole town is going to go crazy!"

Lion looked at Rachel and said, "Why did you lie?"

"What? I'm not lying!" she exclaimed, then looked to the left and to the right. "Once someone sees you everyone is going to start screaming and running for their lives!"

Lion looked at her again. "Why did you lie?"

Rachel put both of her hands on her hips and shouted, "I'm not lying! Don't you get it?"

Lion shook his head and said, "It's you who doesn't get it. Your dad told *you* to cook this morning, not Tomas and Tulie."

She sharply turned her head, looked at him and said, "How did you know that?"

"I know everything. I'm always watching," said Lion.

"What? How?" asked Rachel.

"It doesn't matter how, Rachel. What matters is that you lied. What if your brother or sister gets hurt trying to light the fire to cook? Your father taught *you* how to light a fire. Your mother taught *you* how to cook, not the other children. This is your opportunity to prove that you're growing up, that you're responsible, and that you're trustworthy. Please do what your father asked you to do," proclaimed Lion. Then he turned around and walked away.

Rachel watched Lion walk away as the twins came around the corner and asked, "Who are you talking to?"

Rachel was startled and said, "Oh, no one! I was talking to myself. Don't worry about breakfast. I'll do it. But if you guys can collect all the dirty clothes that need to be washed, that would be very helpful to me."

The twins walked away, shaking their heads and saying to each other, "What's gotten into her?"

It was then that Rachel heard her mother coughing and walked back into the house. She walked into her mother's bedroom and asked, "Are you okay? Can I get you anything?"

Rachel's mother sat up in bed and said to Rachel, "Yes, please. I'd like some water."

Rachel hurried outside and dunked a drinking cup into a large bucket of water. The bucket had flies around it and a thick, green film ran along the edges and down into the bucket; but it was the only water the family had. She filled the cup and quickly walked into the bedroom and handed it to her mother.

"Rachel," her mother said, "I heard you this morning with your brother and sister. Why were you so bossy? That's not how a lady should speak. When I was a little girl I can remember my mother teaching me how to walk straight, tall back and arms free at my side. I remember her telling me how to talk to my elders and how to never talk back. We were always to show respect. I believe I have shown you that too. Why were you so mean?" Rachel looked up slowly and said nothing.

"Rachel, I'm talking to you. Why were you so rude to your brother and sister?"

"I don't know. I can't explain why," she answered.

Rachel's mother put her hand out, and Rachel

took it, stepping in close. Her mother looked at her and said, "Rachel, Tulie looks to you for guidance. You're her older sister. You need to be the example. I know that it gets tiring; I was the eldest in my family too. But it's our job to be a good example. I'm not asking you to be perfect. I'm asking you to be careful. Watch how you act and how you say what you say. She will always look to you! And not only Tulie but Tomas, Joseph, and baby Sophie too. You have to be a model of respect and love."

"I know I was wrong," said Rachel.

"Have you apologized?" asked her mother.

"No . . . They could tell from my voice that I was sorry," she said.

Her mother leaned toward Rachel and said, "They need to *hear* that you're sorry. How are they ever going to learn how to apologize if they don't see it modeled in us? Be a good example, Rachel. They need you and you need them."

Rachel walked out back to where the other kids were playing and she sat there, watching them. Tomas yelled out as he was running around chasing the other children, "Come on! Play with us!"

Rachel smiled, stood up and started chasing the kids along with Tomas. Once all the children were captured Tomas yelled out, "Okay, Rachel and I are going to start counting so you'd better go hide!" So Rachel and Tomas covered their eyes and started counting out loud, "One...Two... Three." Suddenly Rachel stopped counting and opened her eyes. Tomas opened his eyes and said, "Six...Seven," then quieted his voice and said,

"Uh, you're supposed to be counting with me."
Rachel whispered to Tomas, "I'm sorry for being
so bossy this morning." Tomas smiled and yelled,
"Ready or not, here we come!"

4
CHAPTER

The Lie

Now on this particular morning Rachel was excited. She was excited to walk her father to the town's end and to spend time with Lion. She walked into the kitchen dressed and ready to go and was surprised to see her dad sitting at the table with her mother and their neighbor, Nellie, from next door.

"What's going on?" asked Rachel, highly confused.

Rachel's father looked up and said, "Mother

still isn't feeling well and I have to work today, so Nellie is going to take Mother into the next town to see if she can be seen by the clinic doctor."

"But that's far away. It will take all day and even into the night time to get back home," said Rachel who was thinking only about herself and no one else.

"Yes, we know that, Rachel. That's why Nellie offered to take Mother on the back of her mule," said Rachel's father, ignoring Rachel's selfish attitude.

Rachel whined, "So I have to stay home *again?*"

"That's right. You did a great job yesterday. I'm sure that today will be even better," Rachel's father said with confidence.

Rachel's mother wrapped her shawl around

her shoulders as she walked to the front door. She turned around and said, "Rachel, when you prepare the food for today I need you to be very careful with the rice. We have little left and it's very expensive. So please, don't cook it all. You'll probably still be hungry after breakfast and that's okay. When we return I will have more rice to add to the jar. Do you understand?"

"Yes," said Rachel.

Rachel grabbed the container of rice and headed out back to cook the morning breakfast, and, as she looked into the container, she saw that there was very little rice left. She thought to herself, *There's only enough to feed two, maybe three children. How am I going to feed all five?* Rachel's tummy began to growl. So she did just what her mother instructed, cooking only three servings' worth and leaving the last serving in the container. Rachel called the kids over to eat. She portioned out the rice onto each plate. They each looked at their plates, then back at Rachel.

Tomas said, "Rachel, are you crazy? This isn't enough rice to feed a small bird!"

Rachel responded, "I know! Mother said that we were very low on rice and that we would probably be hungry. But when she returns later today, she promised to bring some more."

They all sat there and ate. When they were finished, their tummies weren't content. Tomas jumped up, grabbed the rice container, and announced, "There's still rice in here! If Mother's bringing more, why didn't you cook all of it?"

Rachel stood up and said, "Because, Mother said to leave some rice in the container." Tomas, confused, just walked away with Tulie and Joseph by his side.

Sitting there holding Sophie, Rachel's tummy began to rumble again and the baby started to cry. Rachel sat there rocking Sophie in her arms but she just kept crying. "What should I do? I know you're still hungry." Rachel opened the rice container and thought to herself, *The other kids left to play, and I'm sure that they won't be back for a long time. So what if I cook the rest of this? They'll never know.* So she put Sophie down and began to cook the rest of the rice. She and Sophie ate, and finally the hunger pains stopped, and Sophie stopped crying.

Now, as the sun began to set, Rachel remembered what her mother had instructed her to do, and she grew nervous. She couldn't figure out what to do. So she went out back, looked into the rice container and saw that, yes, it was completely empty. She put her hands on her head, not sure what to do next. First, she took a deep breath and began to pace back and forth. Then, suddenly, she noticed that Nellie had left the back door of her house wide open.

Rachel began to think to herself, *What if I borrow some rice from Nellie, and when Mother gets back with more rice I'll give what I borrowed back to Nellie. Hummm . . .* She walked over to the back door and quietly stepped in. She went straight to the rice container and opened it. Rachel looked into the jar and was very disappointed to find that Nellie's container was almost empty too. She put her head down, not knowing what to do. Then she saw a big bag on the floor labeled,

"Rice." She opened up the bag and filled her container with one serving. She quietly sneaked out the back door with her mother's rice container in her hands.

Just as she was walking out of the back door, there sat Lion.

Rachel was totally surprised and gasped, "What are you doing here? You scared me!"

"What's that you have in your hand?" asked Lion.

"Oh this? This is our rice container. It's pretty, huh?" Rachel said as she tried to evade his question.

"No, Rachel, what is in your hand?" said Lion with a firm voice.

Rachel looked at her hands and said again, with a bit of attitude this time, "It's our rice container, *geez.*"

"What do you have in your hand? I won't ask you again!" Lion said with a strong, forceful voice.

"I have rice! Rice, okay?" said Rachel irritated and arrogant.

"Is it *your* rice?" asked Lion.

"It's in my container, isn't it?" Rachel said sarcastically as she rolled her eyes.

"What were you doing in your neighbor's house? Were you visiting her?" asked the lion, though he knew exactly what was going on.

"Okay, okay! I was borrowing rice from Nellie!" said Rachel acting like a know-it-all.

"Borrowing it?"

Then in a teasing, singing voice, Rachel answered, "Yes, I'm *borrowing* it."

Lion put his head down and said, "Rachel,

you know better than that! You're stealing from your neighbor. A person who borrows asks for permission first! You didn't ask Nellie, you just took it upon yourself to take her rice. Rachel, that's stealing!"

"But she has plenty! She'll never know that it was missing," Rachel argued.

Lion walked up closer to Rachel, sat down, and said, "Okay, what if a family of small birds are working and working hard, trying to collect worms for their babies to eat. And because of their hard work they have a bunch of worms left over so they hide them. They hide them so that they have food for their family when it grows cold. And then suddenly a big black crow sees where they've been hiding their worms, and he goes and takes them away. Is that fair?"

"No, of course not!" said Rachel.

"Why not?" asked Lion

"Because the worms belong to them and not the crows," said Rachel.

"So, is what you've done any different? Is Nellie a hard worker? Does she have a family to feed?" asked Lion.

"I understand," said Rachel, suddenly feeling embarrassed and waiting to hear what she should do next.

"What do you think is the right thing to do at this point?" asked Lion.

Rachel looked up at Lion and said, "I should go and put the rice back and when Mother returns I should tell her and Nellie what I've done."

Lion smiled and told Rachel, "I know it's hard to do the right thing sometimes, but your heart feels better knowing that everything that you do is honest and good. When your mother returns I know that you may be nervous to tell the whole truth. I know that you'll want to fib a little so that what you did doesn't appear to be so bad. But, believe me, your blessing lies in telling the entire truth. Do you understand?"

"Yes," said Rachel knowing that what awaited her would be the hardest thing for her to do.

About an hour later Nellie and Rachel's mother returned home. Her mother was able to see the doctor and everything seemed to be fine. "What's wrong, Rachel? You look ill," said Rachel's mother.

"Um, I have something to tell you . . . and Nellie," said Rachel with a very quiet and meek voice. Then suddenly the front door opened and

Rachel's dad walked into the house from work. Rachel's heart started to race like crazy. *Not my dad. I have to tell him too? He'll be so disappointed,* Rachel thought to herself. Rachel's mother asked her husband to sit down to listen to what Rachel was about to tell them.

"Go ahead, Rachel, you have our attention," said her mother.

"Well," Rachel began to get choked up and her eyes began to fill with tears, "you asked me to only use part of the rice, and I followed your instructions. But Sophie wouldn't stop crying. She was still hungry."

It was in that moment that Rachel thought of a perfect way to put the blame on baby Sophie. She wiped the tears from her eyes because now she had a perfect plan. And then out of the corner of her eye she saw Lion standing in the doorway of her bedroom. She twitched, getting very nervous, her heart began to race even more than before and her tears came flooding back.

"Go on, honey," said her father. She looked back at Lion and he nodded his head.

"Ah . . . I was hungry too! So I cooked the rest of the rice and fed part of it to Sophie and I ate the rest. But after I ate the last grain of rice I remembered what you said and I got nervous. I began to think of what to do. And then I noticed that Nellie's back door was open. So I decided to borrow, I mean steal, some rice from her and replace it later. So I went into her house and saw the big bag of rice, and I took a little bit out. I put it into our rice container and I went home. But I started to feel weird about what I did and my friend told me what I was doing was wrong and asked me what I thought would be the right thing to do next. So I put the rice back and came home."

She looked at Nellie with tears running down her face and said, "Nellie, I'm sorry for walking into your house without asking, and I'm sorry that I stole from you. I promise that I'll never do it again."

Rachel's father looked at Rachel shaking his head. He looked at Nellie, and he too apologized for Rachel's behavior. Her mother stood up and looked at Rachel and said, "Rachel, that's all the rice we had. I didn't have enough money to buy more rice today. I am proud that you were honest, but I'm sad that you were disobedient to my wishes. I asked you to save the last bit of rice so that Sophie could eat tonight. I had to decide who to feed just in case I ran out of money. I knew that we would all go to bed hungry but, if I only had enough to feed the baby, then we'd all be fine."

Rachel dropped her head. Suddenly, Nellie stood up and walked out of the house. They all looked at one another. Was Nellie mad at them? Was she hurt by them? Was she disappointed with them? She walked back into the house with the full bag of rice saying, "Is this the bag you took from?"

Embarrassed, Rachel said, "Yes, ma'am. That's the bag that I took the rice from." Nellie began to giggle. Rachel looked up thinking Nellie had lost her mind. "Why are you laughing?" asked Rachel.

Nellie began to explain, "I work a lot of jobs

just to keep my family cared for and fed. And the other day when I was working at the food shelter, my boss took me into his office and said because of my countless hours of service he wanted to bless me and my family with this bag of rice. I was so excited. Do you know how much money this bag is worth? So I walked home with it and on my way home a group of men tried to steal it from me. But, see, I have this really strong friend and he just happened to be right around the corner and he scared them off. He then told me to share this bag with an honest family and what you just showed me was true honesty, so I'd like to share this bag of rice with you."

Lion walked over to the front door and smiled at Rachel. Rachel eyes welled up with tears. Her mother and father were absolutely excited. Nellie turned around and began to pour half of her bag into the rice container, filling it to the top. Then she continued to fill seven other containers. Her parents were speechless. Nellie tied up her portion of the bag and headed toward the front door. And as she did she looked down at Rachel and said, "Your honesty wasn't about you, it was about feeding your family." And as she walked out of the house she rubbed the head of Lion. Rachel almost fainted! Nellie could see Lion! Lion looked back at Rachel, winked, and walked out behind Nellie.

The Gift

The next morning Rachel jumped out of bed. She had to visit Lion today. So she walked her dad to the town's end and waved good-bye. Then she ran to the hilltop. When she got to the top, Lion was already there.

"*You got here fast,*" he said.

Rachel was out of breath. "I know!"

Lion just laughed, "Why so eager to get here?"

Still trying to catch her breath she said, "I

wanted to know why Nellie could see you but my parents couldn't."

Lion stood up, walked to the edge of the cliff, turned back and looked at Rachel. "Do you remember when those boys were bothering you? Do you remember how there was only one of them who could see me?"

"Yes."

"Do you remember what I told you?"

"You said that it was because he knew you as king and that's why he could see you."

"That's right!"

"But wait," said Rachel, "I'm confused. Why were the other boys able to feel your presence but my parents couldn't?"

Lion walked up to Rachel, sat next to her, and explained, "See Rachel, if a person knows me then they are able to sense me, see me, and hear me. But if they've never asked for me, met me, or looked for me, then they may not even know that I'm in the room."

"So how does Nellie know you?" asked Rachel.

"You'll have to ask her," Lion replied.

"Oh come on! Just tell me," said Rachel.

Lion laughed. "Rachel, that's *her* story. I'll let her tell you." Rachel just stood there staring at him. "Now go on . . . go hear Nellie's story."

So Rachel hurried down the hill and back into town. She went straight to Nellie's work place and saw her sitting out back eating lunch. She plopped down on the bench beside her.

"You finally made it," said Nellie, confident and secure.

"What? How did you know I was coming?" asked Rachel.

"After last night I knew you'd seek me out. You want to know how I met Lion, right?" Nellie said.

"That's exactly why I came," said Rachel, in awe of Nellie's perception.

"Well," Nellie told her. "I was very ill, and I was getting ready to die, and the doctor told my family that there was nothing more that he could do. I was just skin and bones. I couldn't eat without throwing up. I always had a fever, and I was very weak. The doctor said I was sick because of the water I was drinking. It was bad water and the entire town was drinking the same water. People still drink it today."

Rachel's eyes grew big and she said, "Is that why I'm sick? Is that why my mother is sick? Is that why some of my friends and family have died?"

Nellie nodded her head saying, "I'm not one hundred percent sure, but I do believe that's why so many are sick."

"Well, what happened? Why didn't *you* die?" asked Rachel in amazement.

Nellie smiled at Rachel and said, "Well, the doctor left the house and the rest of my family left my room in tears. They just sat in the kitchen mourning. I became angry and thought to myself, *I am very much alive. I'm not dead yet!* So as I laid there I began to cry out. I began to declare healing. I didn't want to die yet. I still had too much to do. My children were too small to fend for themselves and they needed me. I remember shouting, 'Be real to me! I need you!' and out of nowhere there sat Lion at the edge of my bed. I wasn't scared at all. I was in perfect peace.

"He looked at me and said, 'If you believe you're well then get up and tend to your family.' And from that day on Lion and I have been closer than ever."

Rachel's eyes filled up with tears and she asked, "Can Lion heal me?"

Nellie said, "Here, come with me."

Nellie grabbed Rachel by the hand and took her to the opposite side of town. And right outside the town's edge was a small, raised platform, and on it was a pipe coming out from the ground.

Connected to the pipe was an opening and on the other end was a pump. Nellie grabbed an empty bucket, put it under the pipe's opening and began to pump. Suddenly water started running out of the open end. Rachel began jumping up and down saying, "Look, it doesn't have bugs in it or thick green patches in it. It's clear! It's clear! It's clear!" She immediately cupped her little hands and began drinking as the splashing water got her completely wet! She was so happy. Nellie just stood there and smiled, and she saw Lion standing in the distance.

6
CHAPTER

Yes, I Am Ready

That next day Rachel woke up feeling strong and rejuvenated. She changed out of her pajamas and ran out front, excited to cook breakfast. She served her father with joy and took a plate into the room where her mother lay fast asleep. She put the plate on the foot of the bed and walked over to the head of the bed. She softly began to touch her mother's shoulder. And as she did she began to whisper in her mother's ear, "Good morning! The sun is in the sky and the birds are singing you a beautiful song!"

Her mother smiled and opened her eyes and said, "Hey, that's what I always say to you."

Rachel began to giggle and giggle. Her mother, very weak, pulled herself up as Rachel reached for the plate of food. She carefully put the plate on her mother's lap and said, "I made this especially for you."

Rachel's mother looked at her with a tear in her eye and told her, "Rachel, you're such a fast learner! Thank you. I appreciate your effort."

Rachel smiled. "Enjoy! I'm off to walk Father to the town's end." Rachel's mom just smiled as Rachel left the room.

Rachel hurried and hid behind her favorite tree to scare her father again. And sure enough he jumped and she just laughed, grabbing his hand as they began their walk to the end of town. While on their way Rachel's father said, "Wow, Rachel, you're extra happy today. What are you so excited about?"

"Nellie took me to a clean well yesterday and I drank and drank. It tasted *so good*."

"A...a...c-c-clean well," her father stuttered.

"Yes!"

"Where is this well?" he asked.

"It's on the opposite side of town, right past that old wooden fence," exclaimed Rachel.

"The missionary well?" he said, totally puzzled.

"I don't know what it's called. But it's right past that old fence," Rachel repeated.

"That well has been dried up for over ten years," her father said, frowning.

Rachel stopped walking, looked up at her father, and said, "Well, it's wet now!"

Her father believed her. "Rachel, when I return today you must show me this well! This may be just what your mother needs to feel better."

Rachel, still confused, exclaimed, "She's still not feeling well?"

"Honey," her father said with a large lump in his throat, "the doctor isn't sure if it's the dirty water or if it's something else. The medication that's needed is too expensive. The doctor said without the medication she may die soon."

Rachel's lowered her head as great, big tears filled her eyes. Then, she looked up at her father as she remembered Nellie's story. She quickly wiped her eyes and said, "She'll be fine. I have a friend that I know can help. He helped Nellie when she was dying. I'll bring him to the house tonight."

Her father held back his own tears and jumped into the back of the truck. He very somberly waved goodbye to Rachel. She smiled with that amazing smile of hers and waved back.

She turned and started running toward the hilltop. She had to share with Lion what was going on. *He will know what to do,* she thought to herself. When she got to the top of the hill, Lion wasn't there, so Rachel waited. She walked back and forth talking to herself, wondering where in the world he could be.

After a while the hot sun was shining right on top of her and she knew that this was the longest she had ever waited for him. She sat at the edge of the cliff dangling her feet over the edge. She suddenly yelled out over the cliff, "Lion, where are you? I need you!"

"I'm right here," replied Lion with a majestic calm in his voice.

She turned around and started rattling off all these things saying, "You have to come tonight! Father knows that you're coming! You have to heal Mother like you did Nellie! She took me to the well and it was wet again and Father had thought it was dry and, and..." She was completely out of breath. Lion stood up, dropped his head, and tenderly touched his nose to her nose. She suddenly took a few deep breaths and said with tears in her eyes, "Is she going to die?"

Lion lifted her head with his paw and said, "Rachel, she's taught you how to clean, wash, cook,

tend to your brothers and sisters. She's taught you how to love. If she does die, you will be ready and able to get through it, right?"

Rachel's tears grew bigger and were ready to fall as she looked up at Lion and told him, "Yes, I am ready! But Lion, I don't want her to die. How am I going to reach the big jug of oil when the small one is empty? How am I going refill it by myself? Who's going to sing to me when I'm grumpy? Who will rub my tummy when I don't feel good? Who's going to tell me stories at bedtime, and who's going to play with my hair?" Tears began to roll down her cheeks and drip off her chin. Lion softly pulled her in and wrapped his big safe paws around her and let her cry.

"You will be perfectly fine," he said.

Good-bye

Later that night Lion walked down the hill into Rachel's town, entered her home and sat at the foot of her mother's bed. And, as he looked around, Rachel and her father were nowhere to be found. Suddenly Rachel's mother opened her eyes. While she lay in bed looking toward the ceiling, she said, "If you're out there and you can hear me, I'm ready to go. I've been sick for years, trying my hardest not to let the children know of my illness. I have served my home, I have given selflessly, and I have equipped them with the know-how to succeed. Please show yourself and take me home."

Lion walked over to the side of the bed and placed his paw on her hand. She turned and looked at him as tears rolled down the side of her face. "I knew you were here! I could sense you. I've sensed you for a long time. It's funny because every time Rachel's around I feel you."

Lion smiled and said, "Yes, Rachel and I are very close."

"Wait a minute," she said, "*you* are the friend my daughter always speaks of, right? You're the one she hangs out with every morning! You're the one who guides her to the truth, aren't you?"

Lion looked at her and said, "Are you ready to go?"

With a sweet smile she said, "Yes. I'd like to say good-bye to my family first."

Lion walked back over to the foot of the bed, nodded his head and sat there quietly.

Rachel and her father, along with the rest of the children, walked into the mother's room with a bucket of clean water from the well Nellie had led Rachel to. Her father sat on the bed gently lifting his wife's head. Rachel then handed him a cup of fresh water as he began to give his wife a drink. He laid her head back down, knelt by the bed, and said to her, "My Angel, my sweet wife, you are ready aren't you?" as tears began to fall from his face. Rachel and the other children began to cry too.

Rachel's mother opened her eyes, turned her

head to look at them, and said, "A broken heart is an open heart. So stay open to the possibilities of love and peace. Whenever you hear a bird singing, know that it's my voice singing so sweet. Or when you hear a whistle through the trees, let it signify my commitment to all the dreams that I set free. This doesn't have to be a sad moment. It can be a celebration of breakthroughs that are yet to come. But you will have to choose what you will do. My precious husband, you will have to choose strength over weakness. Rachel, you will have to choose courage over fear. Tomas and Tulie, you will have to choose joy over sadness. Joseph and Sophie will have to make their decisions too. So please choose wisely. Your destiny weighs heavily on what you decide!"

She smiled with a sweet glow in her eyes and said, "Yes, I am ready! My body is tired, and we have said all that needs to be said." Her husband reached over and kissed her on her forehead, and with his hands shaking said, "Good-bye! I will always miss you! I will always dream of you! I will always think of you! My life was wonderful with you in it!" He dropped his head onto her shoulder and wept. Rachel stood up and, as all of them began to cry, she ushered the younger children out of the room. As she walked back, her father said to Rachel, "Go now and say good-bye. I will stay out here with the children."

Rachel walked in and saw Lion standing at the foot of the bed. "Wait!" Rachel said as tears continued to flow down her face "Can't you save her? Isn't there anything you can do? You saved Nellie, why can't you save my mother?" Rachel was so confused.

Lion looked at Rachel and said, "Rachel, this is not for you to decide. Your mother is ready to go. You are ready to let her go and in the long run this will continue to make you a powerful woman. You have been created for greatness. Allow this moment to be sweet. Allow this moment to be your gift."

Rachel shouted out, "But!"

She was quickly interrupted by her mother who said with a weak voice, "Rachel, Lion is right." Rachel's eyes grew big as she looked at Lion. Her mother had finally met him. She looked over at Lion and he smiled at her. Her mother continued,

"Grow now. This is your season to grow. I know that you think it's unfair. But you have so many people around you who will help you in those difficult times. Don't be afraid! Don't let fear in! Don't let it have control! You are fearfully and wonderfully made and you can do all things!! So it's your turn to help run the home. My season is over. You will do a great job. I know you will. I have taught you all that I know."

As tears trickled down Rachel's face she climbed into the bed alongside of her mother. Rachel grabbed her mom's arm and wrapped it around herself. Her mother smiled and held Rachel tight. Rachel said in a very weepy voice, "Mother, you are my friend and I will miss our friendship. I will miss your instruction. I will miss your touch;

I will miss our silly songs and twirling time when no one's looking!"

Her mother just patted her on the back and said, "Shh...shh...shh, now, Rachel. It's going to be okay. I would like you to do me a big favor. I'd like you to ask Nellie to watch the children tomorrow and take Father up the hill to meet Lion."

"What? Are you sure?" said Rachel still weeping.

"Yes," said her mother, "it's time that your father meets him. Will you do that for me?"

Rachel looked up at her mother as she lay there in her arms and said, "Yes, I will do as you have instructed."

Lion quietly walked over to the side of the bed and said, "Are you ready now?"

Rachel shouted, "No! No! No! No, not yet!! No, please, please don't go yet, please Mom, please don't leave me!"

Rachel's mother turned to her and held her tightly and said, "Rachel, I will always be here! I will be in the sky in its bright blue and deep grays. I will be in the rising of the sun and the dark of the night. I will be the breeze that touches your face. I will always be there. Just trust Lion.."

As Rachel began to calm down she took a deep breath. She kissed her mom on the cheek and said, "This one is for today." Then she kissed her again and said, "And this one is for tomorrow, and this one is for the next day and the one after that." Rachel continued to kiss her mom over and over again. As her mother closed her eyes as if to go to sleep, Rachel squeezed her one more time, then wiggled out of her mother's arms and stood there saying, "Good-bye mother. I love you."

The Encounter

That morning Rachel awoke very early, earlier than she had before. She sat up and wiped her eyes. She knew it was early because she could see a tiny glare of the black dark sky turning a very bright blue. Her father once told her that's how you can tell that it's morning: when the sun kisses the sky taking the darkness away.

She got up and changed out of her pajamas, remembering what her mother had asked her to do. She began to get excited putting on her shoes, and she jumped up and ran into her parents' room. Her father was lying there completely asleep, eye lids still swollen from all the crying he had done a few hours before. She leaned down and kissed him on his head peacefully saying, "Father. Father, it's me Rachel. Are you awake?"

He carefully opened his puffy eyes and said, "What's wrong Rachel? It's early. Is something the matter?"

"Uh, yes and no," said Rachel.

Her father sat up and said, "What is it?"

"Last night, before mother passed, she asked me to introduce you to my friend. She asked me to do it this morning. So if you don't mind I would like to take you now," said Rachel in a very sweet and soft voice.

"Rachel, I'm sure that your friend is nice and all, but this so-called friend wasn't here last night. Your friend can wait. I'm not exactly in the mood to meet new people," said her father.

Rachel's eyes became a bit watery as she said, "I know. But it's what Mother wanted. I promised her that I would do this! Please, Father, let's go."

She smiled at her father and walked out of the room with confidence that he would follow. She went outside and sat on the swing. Just then she saw Nellie stepping out of her front door. As Rachel watched her she could hear Nellie humming a song that Rachel and her mother always sang together. Nellie closed her front door and began to walk toward Rachel. Nellie looked up and saw Rachel staring at her.

"Why, good morning little one, are you ready for today?" asked Nellie.

"Yes and no! What do I say? Do I say, 'Father this is Lion and Lion this is Father?' What if at that moment Father looks around and doesn't see Lion? What then? I'm confused," Rachel said.

Nellie put her hand on Rachel's head and said, "Let your father call out to Lion. He will. It may not be today. It may not be tomorrow but one day he will. Don't rush him. Let it happen by itself."

"So should I not take Father up to the hilltop?" Rachel asked.

Nellie smiled and said, "No, take him anyway. Let him see where you and Lion hang out. And leave the rest to your father and Lion. Let them encounter one anther in their perfect timing."

Nellie started to walk to the back of the house when Rachel heard Nellie humming that same song again.

Rachel shouted out, "Nellie, where did you learn that song from?"

Nellie looked back at Rachel and said, "Your mother taught it to me just in case you needed someone to sing with!" She turned around and kept walking. Rachel's eyes filled up with happy tears and she smiled. She quietly said, "Mom, if you can hear me, thank you for thinking of me and loving me so much that you would teach Nellie our favorite song. I know that you're gone, but that song makes me feel like you're right here." Just then she heard her dad walk through the front door. She jumped off the swing and looked at him and said, "Great! Let's go."

During their entire walk up the hilltop, her father said not one word. He never questioned anything. He didn't say, "Where are we going? Why are we climbing this hill? Is this a joke?" None of that, he just quietly followed. When they reached the top, Lion wasn't there. So they both sat on the cliff and watched the sun rise.

Then her father said, "I remember meeting your mother for the first time. I was shopping in the market place with my mother. We walked up to a grocer who was selling vegetables, and I asked the young woman how much the produce was and there she stood. She had an amazing smile. You have that same smile. From that point I knew she was to be my wife. My mother even knew it. I put out my hand and I said, 'Hello my name is Salomon.' She smiled and looked down while she put her hand in mine and she giggled saying, 'Hello, it's nice to meet you Salomon. My name is Lilly.' From that point on we purchased our produce from her and her family. That was it! I was sold. My father had about twenty goats, and we offered our best fifteen goats for her hand in marriage. Then we were married.

"I know that it's only been a few hours but I sure miss her!"

Rachel's eyes became full of tears again and

she just sat there quietly. Rachel scooted closer to her father and held his hand while gently laying her head on his arm. He looked down at her and said, "Why did she die?"

Rachel looked up at him and said, "I don't completely understand it either, but Mother said last night that she was ready. I tried to argue with her and my friend, but Mother insisted that it was time."

"Wait," her father said, "your friend was there? I didn't see this so-called friend!"

"Well," Rachel said, "you have to want to see him."

"What? I don't get it," her father said, completely confused.

Rachel looked at her father with her sweet eyes and said, "I didn't understand it either and neither did Nellie or Mother but once they cried out to him, he appeared. I know that it's hard to understand, but you have to want it." Rachel stood up and started down the hilltop leaving her father sitting there alone.

As she got to the bottom of the hill, she looked back and her father was still sitting there. Rachel walked back to her home and when she entered the house Nellie said, "You're back so soon? Where's your father? How did it go?"

Rachel said with a sad look on her face, "I just left him there. If this was going to be his encounter, then I had to let him find Lion on his own. I led him to the place and now it's up to them. It's just like you said, Nellie."

Rachel climbed up Nellie's lap as Nellie wrapped her arms around Rachel. "It's going to be fine," Nellie said.

"I know," said Rachel. "I know."

And she did.

The End
(for now)

Special Thanks

David, Sonia, Hannah & Elijah Lyons, Juan Jr, Rebecca & Levi Alvarado, Mari-Lu Chen, Dyanna de Leon, Fabio & Mercedes Lainez, Miriam Ventura de Porras, and Martin Lainez

Greg & Linda Wallace, Michael Jr & his wife Ebony, Aaron & Patricia Larsen, Nathanael & Michelle Wolf, Brian & Angela Smith, Javier & Eva Arriola, Arturo & Lina Armenta, Joseph & Merisha Talarico, Josh & Chara Swodeck, Marlin & Marlene Munoz, Ruben & Monique Morales, Roberto & Arlene Guzman, Edward & Michilyn Gonzalez, Richman & Debbie Caldwell, John & Rita Ziehr, Tim & Susie Martin, Leo & Cindy Nanez, Chris & Debbie Pipes, Dakri Brown, Jeremiah Woods, Paul Stephens, Siobhan Holmes, Gilda Zavala, Christina Longoria, Kimberly Pauley, Lizsa Pinedo, Grace Wabuke, Nicole Burk, Rai Barrows, Jessica Conrrad, Rebecca Corbett, Renee Loignon, Kerrilie Robertson, Season Roberts, Marcus Maples, Joan Russell, Natalie Allen, Melissa Dabiri, Rosie Calderon, Shannon Johnson, Sherri Bryant, Bania Lopez, Dan McGetric, Dan Asher, Angie Schmidt, Susan Davison, Barbara Salerno, Joy Winans, Rachel Warr, Marianna Dobrovolny, Ashley Greene, Natalie Vesely and Jeff Silberman.

A Heartfelt Thank You To: Juan Alvarado—Dad!! You always leave me in AWE! Thank you for supporting me! Even as a little girl I always knew that I could count on you!! You truly are a man of abundance!! Esther Alvarado—Mom!! Thank you for your honesty and love! I'm wealthy because of you! Rosalinda Alvarado—Tia, Your generosity is breathtaking!! Thank you!! Ramon Alvarado—Tio, Thank you for believing in me! You are a man who I will always honor!

To My AMAZING TEAM!!! Megan Stringfellow, Rosie Grupp, Janice Phelps Williams, Josh Swodeck, Sarah Tse, Deborah Solis and Aldo Padilla—Your level of excellence on this project was spectacular! Thank you for all your love and support!!